First published in the United Kingdom in 2016 by
Pikku Publishing, 7 High Street, Barkway, Hertfordshire SG8 8EA
www.pikkupublishing.com

ISBN: 978-0-9928050-9-8

Text and Illustrations © Markus Majaluoma
Original title: Suu auki, Hulda Pottusammakko tulee!
First published in Finnish by Werner Söderström Corporation (WSOY)

Cover design: Glyn Bridgewater
Translated by Anja Leppanen

F I
L I
Pikku Publishing acknowledges the kind support of FILI in the production of this edition.

1 3 5 7 9 10 8 6 4 2

Printed in China by Toppan Leefung Printing Ltd

OTHER TITLES IN THIS SERIES

Daisy Darling, Let's Have Lunch!

Daisy's Dining Diploma

Daddy's Dining Diploma

A Daisy and Daddy Story Book
Vol. III

MARKUS MAJALUOMA

Pikku Publishing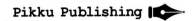

Daisy and Daddy are busy.

It is lunch-time.

Daisy doesn't like carrots.

'Let's mash them up.

Then they'll taste good!' Daddy promises.

'Here comes the carrot train!

CHUG! CHUG! CHUG!' Daddy says.

'What is a carrot train?' Daisy thinks.

Daisy shuts her mouth.

'Here comes the potato pirate...

"Bring me food! Ho! Ho! Ho!"' the villain cries.

'What is a pirate?' Daisy wonders.

And shuts her mouth.

'Here comes the Mash Monster!

MUNCH! MUNCH! MUNCH!' says Daddy.

'What in the world is a Mash Monster?'

Daisy thinks.

And shuts her mouth.

In the wardrobe there is a leek walrus.

'Rrrruuuurrrr!' roars the walrus.

'Why is the walrus in the wardrobe?' Daisy wonders.

She feels very sorry for the walrus.

'Don't cry, my darling,' says Daddy.

He consoles Daisy.

'It wasn't a leek walrus.

It was only me!'

Daddy fetches his tools.

He starts on his new invention.

It is called a Potato Robot.

POTATO ROBOT

The potato sets off.

The potato
loops the loop!

The potato jumps
on the fish slice
trampoline!

Then it leaps
onto a pirate ship…

and drops into the
automatic spoon…

And,
finally…
What
happens?

HURRAH! HURRAH!

Daisy ate a whole spoonful of mashed potato!

Daisy is awarded her Dining Diploma.

'Now we shall make some more healthy mash,' says Daddy.

But Daisy wants to leave her high chair.

Daisy points at Daddy and the Potato Robot.

'What now?' Daddy wonders.

' 'Tato coming! 'Tato coming!' Daisy cries.

Potato mash is good and healthy.

Now it is Daddy's turn to enjoy it.

The End